The Boy Who F█████ His Grandad's Slippers

Words by Billy Bob Buttons   Drawings by Lorna Murphy

For my cheeky little Albert
and his two wonderful sisters

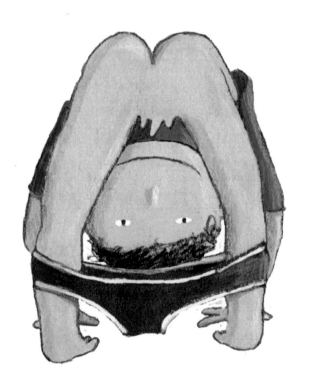

Published by The Wishing Shelf Press, UK in 2016.
Words © Billy Bob Buttons, www.bbbuttons.co.uk
Drawings © Lorna Murphy, www.lornamurphyillustration.com
10 9 8 7 6 5 4 3 2 1

ISBN 978-1514718551

Ralph, a little boy, who just turned three,
Was most happy with no nappy,

FREE
TO
PEE!

He showered bugs and slugs,
Mummy's sheepskin rug,
He filled Daddy's boots and his coffee mug.

But BEST of all,
what he MOST enjoyed...

Was
piddling
on
his
sister's
toys.

Her jigsaw puzzle, her slinky dog,
Her piggy bank and wind-up frog,
Her pink yo-yo, her red lollipop,
He even took a tinkle in her Coco Pops.

TINKLE!

SPRINKLE! SPLASH!

and

SPLATTER!

When Ralph unzips, cats hiss and scatter,
A driving torrent of yellow sleet,
He'd hit Grandad's slippers from...

So they took him to the town GP,
In a bid to cork the gushing wee,
'DOCTOR! HELP!' sobbed Ralph's mummy,
As Ralph spent a penny on the doctor's tummy.

'HORRID BOY!' yelped the doctor.
'Is this a joke?'

But the tiddler just tiddled on her stethoscope.
Then he tiddled on her tuning fork,

And the doctor jumped up with a disgruntled, 'GOLLY GOSH!'
Nurse Bladder sprinted over but slipped in the goo,
Then Daddy turned to Mummy.
'We must be off, it's almost two.'

So off to Piddlington Church they trooped,
To see the vicar, the Reverent Gloop,
'VICAR! HELP!' Ralph's daddy begged,
As Ralph went wee-wee up the vicar's leg.

'HORRID BOY!' yelped the vicar. 'Fetch a mop.'
But the piddler just piddled in his charity pot.

Then he piddled on his cat,

SPLISH!

SPLASH!

SPLOSH!

And the vicar jumped up with a disgruntled, 'GOLLY GOSH!'
Sister Potty thundered over but slipped in the wee,
Then Daddy turned to Mummy.
'We must be off, it's almost three.'

But BEST of all,
what he MOST enjoyed...

Was piddling on his sister's toys.

Her Etch-A-Sketch, her Jack in a Box,
Her spinning top and her cuddly fox,
Her tiddly winks, her red-wheeled truck,
He even took a tinkle on her rubber duck.

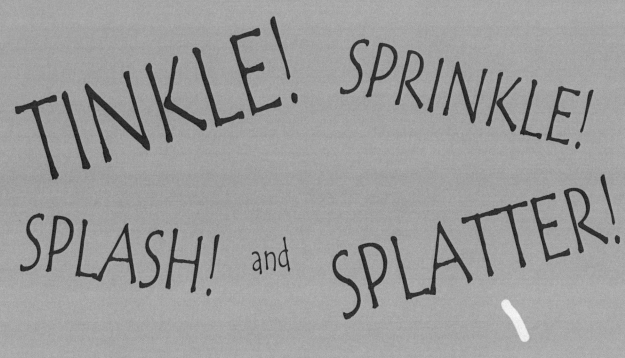

TINKLE! SPRINKLE! SPLASH! and SPLATTER!

When Ralph unzips, cats hiss and scatter,
A driving torrent of yellow sleet,
He'd hit Grandad's slippers from...

When the circus juggler dropped his flaming ring,
A box of rockets blew up with a

BANG!

POP!

ZING!

The puppeteer went crazy,
The unicyclist went nuts!

And the mime pulled down the lid on his imaginary box.

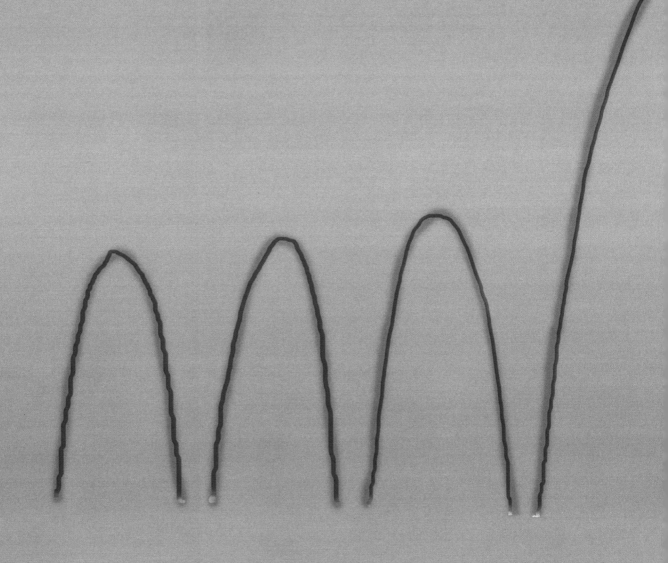

A clown on a pogo stick
threw water on the fire,
But there was confetti
in his bucket,

So the fire...

Then Ralph tottered over, unzipped his zip,
Targeted the rocket box and, with a grin, LET RIP!
The rocket box went SIZZLE! The rocket box shrunk,
The rocket box was soon a soggy box, a soggy box of mushy gunk.

The clowns and the jugglers cheered and clapped,
They danced a wobbly jig and threw up bobbly hats,

THEY SANG...

'He's a bazooker-blasting tiddler,
A volcano-erupting piddler,
An elephant-trumpeting jimmy-riddler,
He's the WIZZKID OF PIDDLINGTON!'

So now when Mummy tells him
not to wet his sister's things,
Not to tiddle on her teddy
or piddle in her bin,

'OK, Mum,' is Ralph's reply,
pulling up his bright-red hood,
'I'm now the WHIZZKID
and I only pee for good.'

But poo's not wet, he pondered, it's just a mushy gloop,
So he jumped up on his sister's bed...

...and did a smelly poop!